Three for Tea

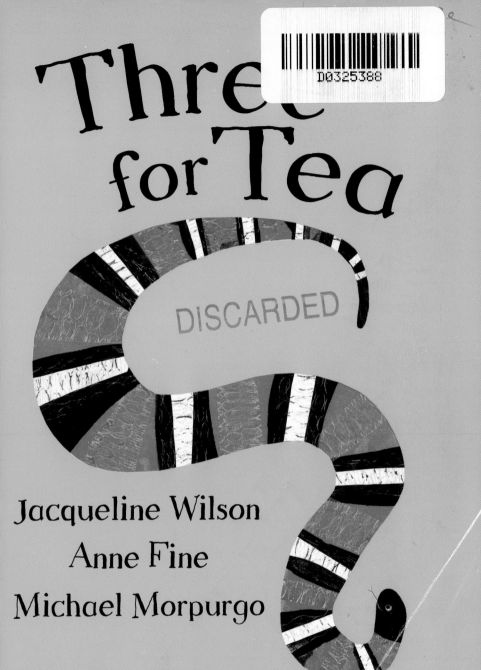

Jacqueline Wilson

Anne Fine

Michael Morpurgo

Tasty Tales
for you and me

EGMONT
We bring stories to life

My Brother Bernadette was first published in Great Britain 1995
Countdown was first published in Great Britain 1996
Snakes and Ladders was first published in Great Britain 1994
Published in one volume as *Three for Tea* 2006 by Egmont UK Ltd
239 Kensington High Street, London W8 6SA

ISBN 978 1 4052 2711 7
ISBN 1 4052 2711 7

1 3 5 7 9 10 8 6 4 2

Printed and bound in Singapore.

Contents

MY BROTHER BERNADETTE

JACQUELINE WILSON

Illustrated by David Roberts

For John Hastings
How Bernard would like
to be in his class!
J.W.

For Paul Harniess
D.R.

Chapter 1

'I DON'T THINK I want to go to this summer project,' said Bernard at breakfast.

'Yes, you do,' said Dad firmly.

'Sara will look after you,' said Mum, putting her arm round Bernard and giving him a cuddle.

I'm Sara. I'm Bernard's big sister and I always get lumbered with looking after my little brother.

'The summer project will be great,' I said, licking honey off my toast. 'There's going to be football and computer games and drama and heaps of other stuff. You'll love it, Bernard,' I said, though I wasn't absolutely sure he would. My little brother Bernard is a bit weird.

'Eat your toast properly, Sara,' said Mum. 'And you eat up too, Bernard.'

Bernard bent over his plate, cutting his toast into tiny little squares, the way he likes it.

'Stop being so finicky, Bernard,' said Dad. 'Come on, if you're quick I'll walk you both over to the summer project on the way to work.'

They've set up the summer project in the school next to our estate. It's being held for a whole month this summer. All the kids on the estate are going. We're all a bit older than Bernard, but Bernard's bright, so they said he could go too.

'I don't want to go,' Bernard said again.

But Dad made him.

'It'll do you good to have a bit of fun,' he said.

A helper took hold of Bernard's hand.

'Cheer up, pal,' he said. 'What would you like to do this morning, eh?'

'I want to play football,' I said. 'Come and watch me, Bernard.'

The helper decided that Bernard had to choose an activity for himself. Bernard didn't want to play football or baseball or judo or trampolining.

'What about model car making?' said
the helper.

'All right,' said Bernard.

My brother Bernard's good at making models.
He's got little Plasticine animals trekking up and
down our bedroom windowsill and his model
aeroplanes zoom above our heads.

Bernard quite fancied the idea of making
model cars. He thought they'd be little cars, but
these model cars were big ones. Another helper
was showing children how to make cars with
wheels and planks of wood. These cars were
big enough to ride on.

Bernard made his own model car with a bit
of help, no problem. He even perched up on
it and went for a very short, slow ride.

But there were a lot of big boys making model cars too. Big Dan was the biggest boy of all. Big Dan is famous on our estate. We all try to keep out of his way.

Big Dan made a big car. He drove it like a dodgem but he didn't dodge. He drove bang into my brother.

Bernard fell off his car. He banged his head and hurt his hands. He tried not to cry but he didn't quite manage it.

The helper picked him up and comforted him. He told Big Dan that he was big enough to know better.

'Poor little Bernard,' said the helper.

Big Dan pulled a terrible face at Bernard.

'Poor little Bernard!' he said, mimicking. 'You stupid sissy little baby. You're like a girl with all that long hair. Bernadette, more like. Yeah. That's your new name. Bernadette.'

Chapter 2

MY BROTHER BERNADETTE didn't like his
new name at all.

'My name's Bernard,' he said. 'Not Bernadette.'

Big Dan kept on calling him Bernadette. So
the other boys did too. Then the girls joined in.
By going home time everyone at the summer
project was calling him Bernadette.

Poor Bernard went very pink in the face.

'His name's *Bernard*,' I said. 'You lot shut up,
do you hear me? Stop calling him silly names.'

I can't stand it when anyone teases my
brother Bernard. *I* tease him sometimes, but
that's different. I'm his big sister.

I'm big but I'm not that big. I'm not anywhere
near as big as Big Dan. I couldn't *make* him
shut up.

'Bernadette,' yelled Big Dan, and ruffled
Bernard's hair and poked him in the chest.
He poked him lots of times, until Bernard fell
over. Again.

I pulled him up quickly, but the helper had seen me and asked if Bernard was all right.

I fidgeted. I know you're are supposed to tell a helper if you are in trouble. I also knew if we told, Big Dan and his mates might get even worse.

'I'm fine, thank you,' said Bernard, in a very small voice.

We could fool the helper, but we couldn't fool Mum.

'Did you fall over, Bernard?' she asked. 'Look at your knees, love! And your hands! And is that a big bump on your head?'

'Yes!' said Bernard.

He was still having a cuddle with Mum when Dad got in.

'Hey there, kids! Did you have fun at the summer project?' he asked eagerly.

'*I* didn't have very much fun, Dad,' said Bernard.

'Big Dan kept pushing him over!' Mum said. 'In fact, they all kept picking on him and calling him names. He's not going back.'

'I don't want to go back,' said Bernard.

But he had to go back. Dad said so.

'He's got to learn to cope with a bit of rough stuff. I think you molly-coddle him far too much. He's got to toughen up a bit,' said Dad.

Mum and Dad had a big argument. Bernard and I crept to our bedroom. Bernie made a Plasticine Big Dan. We dive-bombed him with the aeroplanes. It was fun. Bernard cheered up a bit.

He wasn't so cheerful in the morning.

'Dad says you ought to give the summer project one more try, Bernard,' said Mum.

'I don't want to,' said Bernard.

'You've got to learn how to get on with the other boys, Bernard,' said Dad.

'They don't want to be friends, Dad,' said Bernard.

'This is awful! They're all so much bigger than him!' said Mum. 'Look, he's not going. I'll take the day off work to look after him.'

'You can't keep taking days off work. You'll lose your job,' said Dad.

'Well, maybe Gran could look after him,' said Mum.

'No, it's staying round at his Gran's so often that's turned him into a softie,' said Dad.

Bernard bent his head over his plate and cut up his toast into teeny tiny squares.

'Don't worry, Bernard,' I hissed. 'I'll look after you.'

But I wasn't sure that I could.

Chapter 3

THE CHILDREN STARTED yelling the minute they spotted Bernard.

'Bernadette! Here comes Bernadette!'

Big Dan came swaggering up.

'Ooh look, it's little Bernadette!' he said.

I tried to hurry Bernard away.

Big Dan came after us.

'Here, Bernadette, I'm talking to you.'

'Well, we don't want to talk to *you*, do we, Bernard?' I said.

Another helper came up to us.

'Everything all right, kids?' she said. 'Right, what activity is everyone going to do today?'

'We're going to race our cars,' said Big Dan. 'Wow, pow, wheeee! Come on, guys. Come on, Bernadette.'

Bernard wisely stood his ground.

'What would you like to do today?' said the helper, taking his hand.

'I don't know what I want to do,' said Bernard. 'I know what I *don't* want to do and that's model car making.'

'I think you might well be just the chap for computer games,' said the helper.

But the computer games were so popular that all the places were already taken.

The helper and Bernard mooched around looking for something he wanted to do. I went with him. All my pals called to me to come and join their football team again, but I'd made a promise and I was going to keep it.

'I can't,' I said. 'I've got to look after my brother.'

'How about drama?' said the helper, as we walked past the classroom windows towards the main hall.

'Oh yeah, let's do drama, Bernard,' I said. 'I love acting.'

'I don't think I do,' said Bernard. Suddenly he stopped and peered into a classroom window. 'What are they doing in there?' he asked.

'That's clothes design,' said the helper. 'There's all sorts of jumble sale clothes and ribbon and flowers and stuff, and everyone can design their own creations.'

'*Sewing*!' I said. 'Boring. Come on, Bernard, let's do drama.'

'I want to do sewing,' he said.

'Great,' said the helper.

'You can't do sewing, Bernard!' I said. 'That's for girls.'

'It's for everyone, Sara,' said the helper.

Whatever she said, *I* knew that if Bernard did clothes design every single kid on our estate would call him Bernadette for ever.

Chapter 4

YOU CAN'T ARGUE with my brother Bernard.
He never ever gives in.

Bernard wanted to do sewing. So that's what
he did.

And I did it too. I thought I'd better keep an
eye on him. I felt bad that I'd rushed off to play
football yesterday. There was *one* good thing
about it. Big Dan wasn't going to want to sew.

At least the helper doing clothes design
looked interesting. She had long red hair and a
red dress and an embroidered waistcoat. She
looked up and smiled at us as Bernard and I

went into the classroom. All the other kids looked up too.

'Hey – it's Bernadette,' said one girl, and she and her pal started spluttering as they tried to stop laughing.

'Hello, Bernadette,' said the helper, nodding at me.

I shook my head.

'I'm not Bernadette. I'm Sara,' I said fiercely. 'And this is my brother Bernard. There are no Bernadettes here. And anyone who says there are is going to get beaten up.'

I glared at the girls. They stopped spluttering sharpish.

'Right. Got it,' said the helper. 'Come and sort through the jumble clothes, Sara and Bernard. See if there's anything you fancy. And then there's a bead box here, and some really wacky artificial flowers and there are ribbons and rickrack braid here.'

'Wow,' said Bernard, eyes shining. He started ferreting through the clothes, picking out an old Japanese kimono and stroking its silkiness.

'Don't you dare dress up in that, Bernard,' I hissed.

All he needed now was to start prancing around in a frock!

Bernard sniffed at the idea, but he kept the kimono tucked under one arm.

'Are we allowed to cut some of this stuff, Miss?' he asked.

'Sure,' said the helper. 'That's the whole idea. You two find what you want to work on and then I'll help you pin it and show you how to sew.'

'I can sew already,' said Bernard proudly.

'No you can't,' I said. '*I* can't sew. So you can't either.'

'I can too. Gran showed me how. I sewed on buttons. And I can do over-and-over sewing too. And I expect I can do this sort of picture sewing as well,' said Bernard, fingering the embroidered dragon on the kimono.

My brother Bernard is a little boy but he has big ideas.

He wasn't that good at sewing. The helper suggested we practise a bit on a square of felt. Bernard's stitches were rather big and wobbly. I suppose they were sewing, of a sort.

Better than my stitches actually.

'You're doing well, both of you,' said the helper. 'So you can get started on your actual design now.'

'Bernadette's going to design a dress,' whispered one of the girls.

Bernard's arm went out as he pulled on his long thread. Accidentally on purpose his elbow dug into the girl's side. Bernard's elbows are extremely sharp. Maybe, just maybe, he's learning to look after himself at last.

Chapter 5

I CERTAINLY DIDN'T fancy the idea of making myself a frock. I found some old jeans in the jumble pile and thought I'd cut off the legs and turn them into shorts.

'That's a good idea, Sara,' said the helper.

I went a bit mad with the scissors though. I went chop, chop, chop a little too enthusiastically. And once one leg had gone I had to cut the other one to match.

My shorts were certainly short. They were the shortest shorts ever. So short that they showed my knickers.

'Maybe you could have a little border on them?' said the helper, tactfully.

She got this blue and white check material and helped me cut it out. Well, she did all the cutting, actually. Then she pinned it to the edges of my shorts and sewed a tiny bit to show me how to do it. Then it was my turn. I had to sew. And sew and sew. It was so *BORING*.

Bernard didn't seem the slightest bit bored. He'd found a baseball jacket in the jumble pile. It was too big for him but it looked quite cute on him all the same. It made him look a lot tougher.

'I like it,' said Bernard.

'We can shorten the sleeves a bit,' said the helper.

'I like them long,' said Bernard. 'What I want to do is put a picture on the back. A sewing one, like the pictures on the Japanese dressing-gown thingy.'

'Hmmm,' said the helper doubtfully, but she did try to help. She got some felt and showed Bernard how to embroider a little flower.

'This is a lazy daisy stitch,' she said.

'Lazy daisy,' Bernard repeated solemnly, and had a go. And another and another.

He stitched for an entire hour, until the felt was all grey and sticky, and covered with chains of wobbly lazy daisies.

'Very good, Bernard,' said the helper. 'You can sew some daisies on your jacket now.'

'I don't want daisies,' said Bernard, 'I want a dragon.'

'Ah. Well . . . it would take months of practice before you're at the dragon stage,' said the helper. 'Unless . . . I know!'

She spread the kimono out and carefully cut right round the embroidered dragon.

'Don't spoil it,' said Bernard.

He didn't need to worry. She was leaving quite a bit of edge around the stitches.

'Now!' she said, pinning the dragon into place on the back of the jacket. 'All we have to do is stitch round the edge – and you've got a dragon on your jacket.'

'Great!' said Bernard. It was the sort of over-and-over sewing that Gran had taught him. He was getting better and better at it.

By the time we broke up for lunch he'd finished it. He had an embroidered golden dragon breathing scarlet threads of fire on the back of his jacket. It looked fantastic.

'Look at Bernadette's jacket! I wish I had one like that.'

'Hey, show us how you made it, Bernadette. Can we have a bit of embroidery from the kimono?'

'Will you sew that little Japanese lady on the front of my frock, Bernadette, please?'

The girls gathered round him.

'Maybe,' said Bernard loftily. 'What's my name?'

They soon realised what he meant.

'Bernard. Your name's Bernard. Will you sew my bit first, eh, Bernard?'

Bernard helped them with their sewing all afternoon and I was able to slope off and play football.

I did *not* play football in my new shorts. It would have been my turn to be teased if I had.

Chapter 6

I PLAYED FOOTBALL most afternoons at the summer project, but I went to drama in the mornings. We had a really cracking time, even when Big Dan and some of his gang decided to give it a go too. We had this helper, Len, who was much much bigger than Big Dan.

'You ought to give drama a try, Bernard,' I said. 'It's ever such fun, honest. We're going to do a play for the end of the project. Why don't you be in it too?'

'No thanks,' said Bernard.

'It'll be okay about Big Dan, honest. He's as good as gold with Len. He wouldn't dare call you Bernadette.'

'No one calls me Bernadette now,' said Bernard.

He was right. All the girls in design called him Bernard. Some of the boys called him Bernie or Little Bern. He was getting quite popular. Everyone kept bringing him their old jackets so he could sew something startling on the back. He'd used up every bit of the embroidery on the Japanese kimono, but his helper found some tapestry and an old Swiss blouse and some velvet curtains with a moon

and star pattern. Bernard cut them out carefully
and sorted them out and sewed bits here and
bits there and it all worked a treat.

He even made his helper
a starry waistcoat.

My brother Bernard had
become a little star himself.

'I can't do drama, Sara,' he
said, humming happily. 'I'm
too busy doing design.'

Our drama group asked
Bernard's design lot if they
could help us with our
costumes for our end-of-
project play. We didn't
need anything really fancy,

as the play was about these two tough gangs and how a boy from one gang fell in love with a girl from the other gang.

I was the girl. The main part. I was dead chuffed about that.

Big Dan was one of the rival gang. I was terrified I'd have to fall in love with *him*. Yuck!

Len chose this other boy instead, and said Big Dan had better be the leader of the gang instead. He liked that idea.

Our gang was called the Blue Denims, so we didn't need new costumes, we could just wear our own jeans. Big Dan's gang was called the Black Leathers.

Big Dan came barging into Bernard's classroom.

'Hey, Bernadette, you're supposed to be good at this costume lark. Typical, you little sissy! Anyway, me and my gang need black leather costumes, right?'

'No, it's not all right,' said the design helper. 'You can't come barging in here calling people names and giving orders.'

'It's okay,' said Bernard. 'I'll make you and your gang some black leather costumes, Big Dan.'

'Will you? Yeah, well, good. Thanks . . . Bernadette.'

My brother Bernard simply nodded and smiled.

I thought it was a bit strange.

'I don't know about these black leather costumes,' said the helper. 'No one gives leather to jumbles because it's so expensive. We haven't got any leather and I can't think of anything that looks like leather.'

'I can,' said Bernard. 'Black plastic rubbish bags. Big strong ones so they don't split.'

Everyone thought it was a brilliant idea. It was tricky cutting out pretend black leather jeans and pretend black leather jackets. They glued the seams as there wasn't much time for stitching.

'We could sew some stuff on the back of the jackets, couldn't we?' said Bernard. 'We could use silver thread so it looked like studs.'

It took so long there wasn't time for a dress rehearsal.

'They'll be ready for the performance though, don't worry,' said Bernard.

He took the biggest black plastic jacket home with him and spent hours and hours stitching in secret.

'What are you up to, Bernard?' I asked. 'Why are you taking so much trouble for Big Dan?'

'You'll see,' said my brother and he smiled.

I did see, the next day, when we came to do the play. We all saw.

Bernard handed Big Dan his new black plastic jacket. It was a work of art. Bernard had embroidered hundreds of pink lazy daisies all over it. He'd sewn a message on the back too. *Daisy Dan*.

'I'm not wearing that poncy rubbish,' said Big Dan.

He tried to grab one of the other jackets, but they were all too small for him.

'You'll wear your own jacket,' said Len, forcibly helping him into it, and he pushed Big Dan on stage.

We all fell about when we saw him looking so stupid in his daisy jacket.

'Look what Bernard's sewn for Big Dan!'

'Oh Bernie, you are a scream!'

'Hey, Daisy Dan, I like your flowers!'

No one calls my brother Bernadette any more, but we've all got a brilliant new nickname for Big Dan!

Anne Fine
Countdown

Illustrations by
Tony Trimmer

To Jessie and Leah
T.T.

11:01 AM

HUGO JAMES MACFIE sat on the newspaper spread all over his empty bedroom and asked his father, 'Can I have a gerbil?'

'No,' said his father, painting round the last corner.

'I promise I'd look after it properly.'

'I'm sure you would,' said his father. 'But that's not the point. Think of the gerbil. Think how you'd like to spend your whole life in a cage.'

'I'd let it out.'

'But you're at school all day.'

Hugo counted up on his fingers.

'I'm only out for seven hours.'

His father painted over the last of the yellow with the new blue.

'It's long enough to sit in a boring old cage all by yourself, with nothing to do.'

'I could give it things to play with while I'm gone.'

'That might not be enough to keep it happy.'

'It would be clean and safe and comfy, though.'

His father looked round the four freshly painted walls.

'This bedroom's clean and safe and comfy,' he said. 'A perfect cage, in fact, for someone your size. But you wouldn't want to spend seven hours in here, all by yourself.'

'I'd be all right.'

His father dropped the brush into the can. 'Prove it,' he said. 'Spend the day here.'

Hugo looked round the empty room. 'The whole day?'

'Seven hours,' his father said. 'The time you'd usually be out at school.'

Hugo looked at his watch. It was eleven in the morning.

'Start at noon,' said his father. 'Spend the next hour getting organised, then see if you can stick it. Midday until evening. Twelve o'clock till seven.'

'And if I do it, can I have a gerbil?'

His father picked up the paint rags. 'If you can do it,' he said, 'I'll not just bring your furniture back in. I'll bring a gerbil, too.'

'Synchronise watches,' said Hugo. 'I make it exactly eleven-o-four.'

Mr MacFie set his watch.

'Eleven-o-four. One plate of food. One bottle of water. Three of your old toys. And all the newspaper that's spread over the floor. Is that a deal?'

'See you at twelve,' said Hugo. 'Ready to go.'

11:58 AM

MR MACFIE CLOSED his hand round the door knob and inspected his watch.

'Ready?'

Hugo checked everything: his water bottle here, his food plate there, and the three things he'd taken from the toybox spread out in front of him on the floor.

'Ready,' he told his father. 'Lock me in.'

'Certainly not,' said his father. 'You know that's totally against my principles.'

He shut the door.

12:01 PM

HUGO LOOKED ROUND what he now thought
of as his nice new cage. Soft breaths of air
waltzed through the open window. The one
bare lightbulb hung from the matt white ceiling.
The walls shone perfect Harebell Blue. Across
the floor lay a square sea of newsprint. On top
of that lay the three things he'd borrowed from
Charlotte's toybox.

1. The dancing monkey on a stick.

2. Wee Grey Ghostie.

3. The box of baby bricks.

He'd taken the monkey on a stick because Charlotte wouldn't let him touch it usually. He'd chosen Wee Grey Ghostie because she was his favourite puppet when he was young. And he'd picked up the brick box because he'd heard his mother say a thousand times that you could fill a child's room with expensive toys, but when it came to keeping them busy for hours and hours, you couldn't beat a box of bricks.

So. Was she right?

He built a tower.

Then he built a house.

He built a viaduct. And then a rather fancy
archway that fell down.

And then a prison wall.

Then he was bored.

He took Wee Grey Ghostie and made her
peer over his prison wall. She looked this way
and that.

'Whooooo,' he made her say. 'Whooooo.
Whooooo. Whooooo.'

Then he was bored.

He took the monkey on a stick and made it
flip over and over.

'Hi, Ghostie,' he made the monkey say.

'Whoooo,' said Wee Ghostie.

'Look at me.'

'Whooooo.'

'Backward flip. Up and over. Hanging in
the air.'

'Whooooo.'

Wee Grey Ghostie couldn't help sounding bored.

Hugo MacFie packed the bricks back in their box and laid the puppet ghost on top. He leant the monkey on a stick against the lid.

As soon as he got out, he'd tell his mother she was wrong. A box of bricks was just as boring as a puppet ghost and a monkey on a stick.

How long was that, then?

Hugo studied his watch.

12.31.

Just under six and a half more hours.

HE READ THE newspaper. It wasn't easy. Great splatters of paint had fallen from the ceiling, making it difficult to read. *New rules for banks* he managed to make out. Then *foreign sales on the up and up.* Boring. *Shares plunge after fears.* But fears of what was now a big white blob. He tried to pick it off, but only tore the paper.

He tried another patch.

Massive deposits . . . divided by the share price.

Boring in spades.

He crawled across the floor, nose to the
paper. There it was, all around him: business
news. Nothing worth reading. No *KILLER SHARK
EATS FAMILY OF FOUR*. No *WIND SNATCHES
WIG OFF BEAUTY QUEEN*. No *MORE HAUNTED
HOUSE HORRORS – See pages 4–11*. When he
grew up, he'd buy a proper paper, not the
Financial Times. He'd speak to his father about
it the moment he got out of here.

When would that be?

Hugo looked at his watch.

In six hours and twenty-one minutes.

Less than an hour gone. It seemed like *weeks*.

12:42 PM

SO WAS HE hungry yet? Hugo had a little think.
He wasn't hungry yet. He'd had a proper
breakfast. Then, just in case, an early lunch. His
orange sat on the plate. His sandwich waited.
And his three chocolate biscuits lay in a pile. He
planned to eat his snack at four-thirty. Then,
when he got out at seven, he'd have the supper
his mother promised to keep warm.

That was the plan. He studied the plate again.
Orange. Sandwich. And two chocolate biscuits.
Hugo stared. Where had the third one *gone?*

Guiltily, he brushed the biscuit crumbs off his
chest. He hadn't even noticed
he was eating it.

Only 12.44.

What a *waste*.

If he'd been thinking
properly, he'd have
taken more time.

12:47 PM

HUGO ROCKED GENTLY back and forward on
the floor. The walls swayed with him, blue as
sky. Sky all around. No, *sea*. Sea all around him.
He was on a raft. A speckled, printed raft. The
blobs of paint were droppings from the gulls.
No land in sight. Nothing but sea for miles and
miles. Perhaps a dolphin would come. Maybe a
whale. Or even sharks. What was that strange
shape over there that looked like a paint scraper
on the floor, but could as easily be . . .

Shark!

Sending the sandwich flying, Hugo snatched up the plate and paddled with all his might.

'Save me!' he whispered frantically through gritted teeth. 'Oh, save me, someone! Is there no-one there?'

Around him, the seagulls cried. The lightbulb sun beat down. And the soft zephyrs crept over the sill, over the waves and raft, cooling his fevered brow.

He paddled desperately.

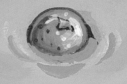

'Oh, for a sight of land! Six weeks! Six
desperate weeks adrift. My stores so low that I
have only a sandwich, an orange, and two ship's
biscuits left. If no vessel passes, I shall surely
die!'

His paddling grew more frantic.

'Help!' he cried. 'Help me! – Oh, oh, help!'

But no help came.

Hugo paddled onward through the waves
until, discouraged and exhausted, he lost hope,
and ate his only sandwich.

12:59 PM

NATURALLY, AS A man will, stuck on a burning ocean on a raft, he soon went mad.

'Ghostie,' he whispered. 'Ghostie, can you remember back when you were mine?'

Wee Ghostie nodded. How could she forget?

'And you were white?'

Forlornly, Wee Ghostie hung her head.

'Well,' Hugo confessed. 'You know that day Mum stuffed you in the washing machine by mistake, and I sat and watched you going round and round, until you went grey?'

Wee Ghostie nodded again.

'That was my fault,' admitted Hugo. 'I was the one who dropped you in the laundry basket by mistake. If I'd done what I was told, and sorted the laundry more carefully, you wouldn't have gone all lumpy and grey.'

Wee Ghostie hung her lumpy head.

'Sorry,' said Hugo. 'I am really sorry.'

Wee Ghostie said not a word.

'Still,' Hugo said, cheering suddenly. 'I feel a whole lot better, just for telling you.'

Wee Ghostie stared.

01:03 PM

HUGO LEANED OUT of the window as far as he
dared. If he could slip his hand around the
metal strut holding the gutter up, then he could
swing across to the drainpipe. Then he could
shin down that as far as the tree, and, if the big
branch held, he could slide down to Mr Foster's
wall, crawl along that, and let himself down on
the dustbins.

Or he could rip his clothes into long shreds and knot them tightly together, like a rope, and tie it to the window catch. Then he could slither down and jump, trying to make sure he missed the rosebush, and land on the grass, next to the cat's bowl.

Or he could climb up on the guttering, balance along and then crawl up the roof, over the top, and down the other side, on to the porch.

Or he could just walk out the door, of course . . .

But not for – he studied his watch – five hours and fifty minutes.

He watched the numbers on his watch face flash and change.

Five hours and forty-nine.

He watched them change again.

Five hours and forty-eight.

A gerbil wouldn't have a watch, of course, to count the minutes pass. All that a gerbil could do was prowl around his nice new cage.

HUGO PROWLED ROUND his nice new room. The smell of paint was strongest in the corner that Dad had painted last. Sunlight fell firmly on the furthest wall, making the blue look lighter. When the sun dropped behind the tree there might be shadows he could watch to pass the time. But not until then. And that would be hours.

01:17 PM

HUGO PICKED UP the orange and tossed it in
the air.

Once.

Twice.

Again.

Then, bored, he sniffed at it.

The smell of orange peel was sharper than
he'd thought. He scraped with his nail to make it
smell even more strongly, then he lay down and
held the orange to his nose.

Now he was lying underneath an orange tree. He was in Spain. If he opened his eyes he'd see the terrace and the swimming pool. He'd inch his way across the burning tiles and slither over the edge, into the crystal water. The cooling blue would close over his head and he would twist and turn under the sunlit droplets.

Splash, splash!

Free as a fish!

No. He was an eagle now. From way, way up, he'd spot the orange peeking from its branch, and swoop down, from sheer high spirits, to knock it from the tree. The sharp fizz taste would smear his beak and send him wheeling up again, into high skies.

Flap, flap!

Free as a bird!

01.26.

But he was here, under a matt white ceiling, trapped in on all four sides by Harebell Blue walls. Beneath him lapped, not silken water, but the grubby old *Financial Times*.

On holiday, his father said, a dozen times a day: 'This is the life!'

And this, thought Hugo, definitely wasn't.

01:29 PM

FIRST HE RIPPED out the word *HELP*. (He
found it in a headline: *HELP FOR SALES*.) Then
he tore gently round the *ME* (in *MERCHANDISE*).
He found an *I* (in *INTEREST RATES*), an *AM* (in
AMERICAN SHARES), the letters *TRA* (in *TRADE
FIGURES*), a spare *P* (in *PENSIONS*), and then a
PED (in *PEDESTRIAN PRECINCT*).

He found the thickest blob of paint (just above

HELP Me I AM traP PED

SCOTTISH WORKFORCE SLASHED) and picked it off. It was still sticky, luckily. He used it to glue his message to the blankest patch of paper he could find (which was a bit of bare wall in the photo of the Manager of Tesco's).

His fingers were covered with matt white, but he'd done it.

What did he need now?

An empty bottle, of course.

Hugo tipped back his head and drank his water, every drop of it. He rolled his message up and pushed it in. Then he crawled to the door.

Footsteps!

He definitely heard them coming up the stairs. Was it his mum? Or his dad? It couldn't be Charlotte. She was still at Granny's house. He put his ear to the door.

Thud, thud.

His heart beat with excitement.

Thud, thud, thud.

The steps drew nearer. Then they passed the door. He heard a rattle further along the landing. Someone was going into his parents' bedroom now. It could be either of them. Hard to tell.

He waited, his ear pressed up against the door, for quite a while. And then he heard the whole performance again, but in reverse.

Rattle.

Then *thud, thud, thud* along the landing – *right* outside his door!

Then *thud, thud,* down the stairs, fading away.

Hugo leant back against the door, exhausted from the excitement.

It was the most dramatic thing that had happened in – Hugo studied his watch – nearly two hours.

01.56.

01:59 PM

'RIGHT,' HUGO TOLD his brain firmly. 'Stop thinking. Empty yourself. Go blank. Go totally blank.'

Right at the back of his brain, a silent voice reminded him sharply:

'Let's not forget our manners. Try saying "please".'

'Please,' Hugo thought to himself. And then he wondered why he felt obliged to suck up to one small bit of him. You wouldn't say 'please' to a toenail, would you? Or to a knee? Why should your brain get all the fancy treatment? Was it fair?

Hugo tried unsaying 'please'.

'I didn't mean that,' Hugo told his brain. 'It doesn't count. We're starting off again.'

He took a deep breath.

'Right,' he said. 'Stop thinking. Empty yourself. Go totally blank.'

'You mind your manners, Hugo,' said his brain.

'My manners are none of your business.'

'I think they are,' his brain said loftily.

'Who says?'

'I do.'

'But you're just me. You're nothing but my brain. And if it weren't for me, you wouldn't be here, would you?'

'And if it weren't for me,' his brain said nastily, 'you wouldn't be here either. So snubs to you.'

'And snubs to you.'

'With big brass knobs on.'

'And with double return.'

Hugo jumped to his feet.

'I'm going mad!' he said aloud.

'Serves you right!' crowed his brain.

'Shut up!'

'Shut up yourself.'

'You shut up first.'

'No, *you*.'

'You started it.'

'I certainly did not.'

And Hugo knew his brain was right. He'd started it himself by trying to tell his brain what it should do.

'Pax?' offered Hugo.

'Pax,' agreed his brain.

It took a bit of time and both the chocolate biscuits, but in the end the brain piped down in Hugo's head.

By 02.09, he felt himself again.

HUGO SANG *Flower of Scotland* to the lightbulb
at the top of his voice. Then he sang *When my
Sugar Walked Down the Street* (his father's
favourite), then a short medley from the book of
nursery rhymes he'd been forced to pass down
to Charlotte. Then he sang telly jingles. Then the
theme song from *The Flintstones*. Then the first
verse – all that he could remember – of Granny's
favourite hymn: *The Head That Once Was
Crowned With Thorns*.

Then he sang *Flower of Scotland* all over again. Then he was bored, and sat twiddling his thumbs, waiting for the end number to change on his watch face.

02.30; 02.31; 02.32.

He lost track of time for a bit – 02.37, then tried, unsuccessfully, to pick the last of the sticky white paint off his fingertips. Then he

lay back and imagined himself drowning. Down, down into the salty darkness he would go, through all the folding billows of the sea, his hair rippling like weeds, his eyes ablaze like underwater headlamps.

He sat up and looked at his watch.

02.41.

02:43 PM

HUGO JAMES MACFIE took a quick vote on it.
The monkey on a stick was all for giving up at
once. Wee Grey Ghostie was happy either way.
And Hugo didn't give the bricks a say.

The lightbulb stared down dispassionately as
Hugo announced the official result.

'In favour of staying: none. In favour of
leaving: two.'

That was settled, then. They were leaving.
Hugo picked up his two companions
(abandoning the bricks) and walked to the door.

He checked his watch face as he opened it.

02.47.

He bumped into his father on the stairs. His father looked at him. Then he looked at Hugo's fingertips.

'I hope you haven't left sticky white fingerprints all over my freshly painted walls,' he said.

Hugo ignored him.

Mr MacFie gave his son another long, steady look. Then: 'Would you like me to help you carry your stuff back in?' he asked.

Hugo shook his head firmly. 'No, thank you,' he told his father. 'Not right now. I thought I'd go outside and play.'

'A wise decision,' said his father gravely.

He stood and watched as Hugo James MacFie went down the stairs and out of the front door, into the wind and sun.

02:49 PM – THE END.

Snakes
and
Ladders

Michael Morpurgo

Illustrated by Anne Wilson

Chapter One

SOME PEOPLE HAVE goldfish or tortoises or hamsters. Wendy's grandad had a snake, a King-snake called Slinky. He was black and gold with little beady eyes and an ever-flicking forked tongue.

Slinky lived in a glass tank on top of the chest-of-drawers in Grandad's bedroom. And that, said Wendy's mother, was exactly where he had to stay.

If Wendy wanted to play with Slinky, then she had to do it in Grandad's bedroom and SHUT THE DOOR.

Wendy was small and thin and quiet.
Hopscotch and handstands were never her idea
of fun. So at school they called her 'weedy
Wendy'. Sad stories made her cry, and so did
Simon McTavish when he kept teasing her about
being poor or about not having a father. So they
called her 'weepy Wendy'. She hated school,
and most of all she hated Simon McTavish.

When she got home from school her mother was out at work like she always was and Grandad was still out in his garden. She sat on the bed in Grandad's room and told Slinky all about Simon McTavish and the horrible things he'd said that day. 'And anyway, we're not poor,' she went on. 'And I have got a dad. He just doesn't live here any more, that's all.'

Slinky flicked out his tongue, which was his way of asking for his tea. He always had a mouse for his tea, a dead one, of course.

When he'd finished swallowing it, Wendy wrapped him round her neck like a scarf and stroked him in between his eyes where he liked it. She hummed him his favourite tune, a jingle from the television, the one about the washing-up liquid that keeps your hands soft.

Grandad came in from the garden. He loved his garden, especially his vegetables. The garden backed on to the park, so he could lean on his fork and watch the football whenever he felt like it. He loved his football almost as much as his garden.

'That cauliflower will be perfect,' he said, wiping his hands on a towel. 'By the time I get back, it'll be just right. We'll have it for Christmas.'

'Why, where are you going?' Wendy asked.

'Hospital,' he patted his side. 'New hip. Nothing to worry about. The old one's worn itself right out.'

Chapter Two

NEXT DAY THEY took Grandad into hospital on the way to school. Wendy's mother was silent with worry. Grandad tried to cheer her up, but it didn't work. He turned to Wendy.

'Now, my girl, you will look after Slinky for me, won't you? No tit-bits, mind. Just his two regular mice, one for his breakfast, one for his tea. And keep an eye on my cauliflower. Any sign of frost, cover it up.'

The car came to a stop.

'I'll see myself in,' he said, and he was gone. Wendy's mother never said a word all the way to school. The first person Wendy saw at school was Simon McTavish. He was roaring around the playground whirling his bag above his head. Wendy took a deep breath and walked into school hoping he wouldn't notice her.

'Now then, children,' Mrs Paterson began. 'I've had an idea. And where do I always have my best ideas?'

'In the bath,' they chorused.

'Quite right,' she laughed. 'Well now, I was in my bath last night and I was wondering what we should do for the Parents' Evening this Christmas. Year Three are doing the Nativity play this year. Year Four are cooking the mince pies and Year Five are decorating the hall. What shall we do? I know, I thought, Year Six will put on an exhibition of "Interesting Things" in the front hall, so that people will have

something to look at while they're eating their mince pies. Well, what do you think?'

Simon McTavish pretended to yawn noisily, but she ignored him.

'Well then, why don't we all try to bring in something really interesting, something from the past maybe, something from a far-off country, something amazing, something special.'

Mrs Paterson did go on a bit, but Wendy liked her because she laughed a lot.

'Now, can anyone think of something they'd like to bring in?' Mrs Paterson asked. 'Sarah, what about you?'

Sarah said she had a three-legged milking stool. Sharon had a telescope and Vince said he'd bring in a fox's tail.

'And how about you, Wendy?' she said.

There was only one thing Wendy could think of.

'We've got this old war helmet, Miss,' she said. 'It's my grandad's. He had it in the war. It's a bit rusty though.'

'Like your grandad then,' said Simon McTavish and everyone sniggered. Wendy felt the tears coming.

'A helmet will be just fine, Wendy,' said Mrs Paterson quickly. Then she turned to Simon. 'And Simon McTavish, you've got a brain like a soggy Weetabix.'

Now they were all laughing at Simon instead, and Wendy suddenly felt a lot better. But for the rest of the day she kept finding Simon McTavish looking at her. There was a very nasty smile on his face.

Chapter Three

GRANDAD HAD HIS hip operation the next
day. Wendy's mother rang the hospital that
evening to find out how he was. He was fine
they said, still a bit woozy, but doing well.
They went in to visit him the following
evening. He didn't look very well to Wendy.
He was thin and pale, with one tube in his
arm and another one up his nose. But he
seemed happy enough.

'All done,' he said. 'Good as new. I'll be
playing football inside a week. How's Slinky?
Haven't you brought him in to see me, then?'

And they all laughed at that. Wendy liked to
see her mother laugh. She didn't laugh much
these days, not since Dad had gone away and
left them.

Wendy remembered to ask Grandad about
borrowing his helmet from the war.

'Course you can,' he said, 'just so long as
you look after old Slinky like I said, and my
cauliflower.'

'Promise,' said Wendy.

That evening she told Slinky all about
Grandad and his tubes. She fed him his mouse

and hummed him his tune and wrapped him around her neck. She stroked him between the eyes, and told him some of the interesting things the other children were bringing in, like Bindi's wooden elephant and Paul's baseball bat.

'But,' she said, 'no one's got a helmet like Grandad's. I'm going to clean it up a bit and then take it into school tomorrow. It'll be the best thing there, you'll see.'

By the time she got to school in the morning, with the helmet in her bag, there was already a huge crowd in the cloakroom. Simon McTavish was there. He stood up on the bench and smiled at her as she came in, only it wasn't a real smile. Then he bent down. When he stood up again there was a helmet on his head, not a battered old rusty war helmet, but a gleaming yellow firefighter's helmet.

'Well, Weedy, what d'you think?' he said. 'My dad collects them. We've got four more at home. But then, some of us haven't got dads, have we?'

She turned away and took off her coat before they could see she was crying.

She told Slinky all about it that evening
when they came back from seeing Grandad
in the hospital.

'That Simon McTavish, he did it on purpose,
I know he did,' she said fiercely. 'I could kill
him, Slinky, I really could. I mean, what would
Grandad's rusty old thing look like next to his?
They'd just laugh at it. I left it in my bag. I never
showed anyone. I told Mrs Paterson I'd changed
my mind. I think she knew, though. She's not
daft. I said I'd bring in something else tomorrow,
but I haven't got anything else, have I?'

108

As she was speaking, Slinky was looking right into her eyes. He was trying to tell her something.

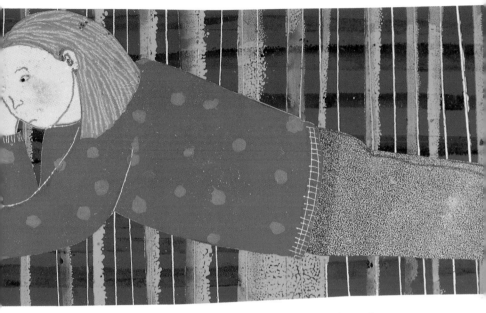

'What about me?' he was saying. 'Why don't you take me?'

Mad, she thought. Ridiculous. Then she thought again. No, it wasn't. It was brilliant. It was the most brilliant idea in the world! She laughed, kissed Slinky on his nose and made up her mind. She would wait until the morning of the Christmas Evening and then take Slinky with her into school.

Chapter Four

BY THE TIME the great day came Wendy had it all worked out. She gave Slinky his breakfast. Then she had her own. She picked up her red lunch-box from the kitchen as usual. Once in Grandad's room, she put her lunch-box in her bag and curled Slinky around it carefully.

'You're not to move,' she whispered, as she closed her bag and buckled it up.

All the way to school she sat in the back of the car and hugged her bag close. Her mother was talking to her over her shoulder.

'Grandad's coming home tonight,' she said, and she wiped the steam off the windscreen. 'I'll bring him along to the Parents' Evening if he's well enough. Did you feed that horrible snake this morning?'

Wendy was thinking it was a good thing that snakes didn't bark or quack or squeak.

'Your dad couldn't stand snakes either, nor spiders come to that. And what do we end up with? Snakes in the bedroom and spiders in the bathroom. No wonder he ran off! Still, we manage, don't we, dear?'

'Course we do, Mum,' said Wendy, and they smiled at each other in the rear-view mirror. They pulled up outside the school gates.

Wendy left her bag hanging up with her anorak in the cloakroom. It would be safe enough till Assembly was over. Assembly was all Christmas carols, and then Mrs Green, the Headteacher, told everyone to have a look at Year Six's wonderful exhibition. The hallowe'en pumpkin was wearing a firefighter's helmet, she said. And there'd be lots of other surprises. More than you know, thought Wendy, more than you know.

Simon McTavish thumbed his nose at her from across the hall.

'You just wait, Simon McTavish,' she said under her breath. 'You just wait.'

As soon as Assembly was over she raced back to the cloakroom. She knew at once that something was wrong. The bag was light, far too light. She looked inside. Slinky was gone, but not all of him. He'd left his skin behind.

Wendy searched everywhere, under the benches, in the toilets, everywhere.

'Wendy, I've been looking for you all over.'

It was Mrs Paterson. As they walked together along the corridor, she said:

'And did you bring something for the exhibition, like you said you would?'

'Yes, Miss,' Wendy said, still looking around her. He couldn't have gone far. He couldn't have.

She was at her table still clutching her bag when Mrs Paterson clapped her hands.

'Now then, children,' she began. 'Wendy has something for us, haven't you, Wendy?'

All heads swivelled. All eyes were on her.

She opened her bag. It was either the red lunch-box or the snakeskin. She picked up Slinky's cast-off skin and held it up between thumb and forefinger. Simon McTavish was laughing like a drain, and so was everyone else, except Mrs Paterson.

'That is wonderful,' she said. 'A snakeskin, a real snakeskin.'

The laughing stopped.

'That's the most wonderful thing we've had. And do you know why? Well, I'll tell you.

Because it's a miracle of nature, a real wonder of the world. Where on earth did you get it from, Wendy?'

She shrugged her shoulders.

'I just found it,' she said, liking Mrs Paterson more than ever. She'd even stopped worrying about Slinky. She'd find him in break. He'd be curled up somewhere asleep. He'd be all right.

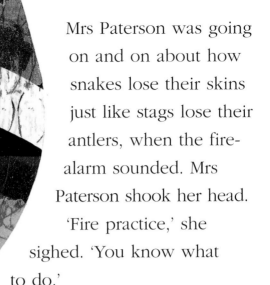

Mrs Paterson was going on and on about how snakes lose their skins just like stags lose their antlers, when the fire-alarm sounded. Mrs Paterson shook her head. 'Fire practice,' she sighed. 'You know what to do.'

They lined up in the corridor and walked out into the playground where they all stood in long cold lines waiting to be counted.

The teachers were gathered in a huddle around Mrs Green who was talking in an animated whisper just loud enough for Wendy to understand most of what she was saying.

' . . . yes, I am quite sure . . . in the cloakroom . . . but it could be anywhere by now . . . could be deadly. Yes, of course I've rung the police . . . Now, I want the children counted carefully and I want all the doors

locked . . . that way no one can get in and
he can't get out . . . '

The teachers ran off in all directions, except
Mrs Paterson who was talking into Mrs Green's
ear. Both of them were looking at Wendy now,
and then they were coming straight towards her.

'Wendy dear,' said Mrs Paterson. 'That snakeskin you brought in this morning. You told me
you found it.'

'Yes, Miss.'

'Well where did you find it, Wendy?'

'Over by the hedge,' said Wendy, thinking as fast as she could. 'Over there.'

But Mrs Green was still worried, very worried.

'Wendy,' she said, 'you didn't actually touch the snake, did you?'

'No, Miss,' she said. Lying, Wendy thought, is quite easy when you have to. 'I never even saw it, Miss. Just the skin. Honest.'

Mrs Green seemed relieved at that.

She spoke now to everyone.

'Children, we are going to have to stay out

here for just a few minutes more. There is nothing whatsoever to worry about, nothing at all. Now why don't we all sing a nice carol to keep ourselves warm?'

They were half-way through 'In the bleak mid-winter', when some of the Infants stopped singing and began to point up at the big chestnut tree by the playground wall. Something was moving high in the branches, something black and gold, and slinky. Someone screamed, and then everyone was shouting and screaming and running. They ran as far from the tree as they could go, as far as the boundary hedge. The teachers rushed over and tried to calm them and comfort them. Only Wendy stayed where she was. Now she had found Slinky, she wasn't going to let him out of her sight. She could hear the police sirens now, but she kept her eye on Slinky all the time.

Chapter Five

TWO POLICE CARS came first, then a fire engine. Flashing and whining, they drove straight through the school gates and into the playground. Police and firefighters leapt out.

Wendy listened hard as Mrs Green explained everything to the police officer, who nodded and then mumbled something Wendy couldn't hear into his radio. He was looking up at Slinky, shielding his eyes against the sun.

'I don't like the look of him,' he said. 'Black and gold. Could be poisonous. I'm not taking any chances, Mrs Green, not with my officers, not with your children. You'd best take the children back inside the school where they can't see. He may have to be shot.'

'No!' Wendy cried. 'No!'

And before anyone could stop her she was up on the playground wall and running along it towards the tree.

She grabbed an overhanging branch, swung herself up and began to climb.

They were shouting up at her to come down,
but she kept climbing.

The higher she climbed the more branches
there were, and the easier it was – until she
looked down. Everyone was so small. The fire
engine was a toy.

Then she saw a policeman with a rifle. He
was aiming at the top of the tree.

'Don't shoot!' she screamed. 'Don't shoot!'
And she climbed again.

When at last she reached Slinky, he was
curled around the highest branch and would
not let go.

'I won't let them hurt you,' she said, stroking
him between the eyes. 'Honest I won't.'

And she hummed him his favourite tune

as she prised him off the branch and wrapped him round her neck. Then the wind blew and the tree swayed and she felt suddenly sick with fear. She clung to the branch and tried not to look down. But she did look. There was a ladder up against the tree, and a firefighter was climbing up towards her.

'Don't move,' he called to her. 'I'm coming. I'm coming.' His face was paper-white under his yellow helmet.

He went on talking as he climbed off the ladder and into the tree.

'What's your name, then?'

'Wendy.'

'Nice name.' He was getting closer all the time. 'I'm Peter, Peter McTavish. My boy Simon, he's in your school. You know him?'

'Yes,' said Wendy. 'I know him.'

'Little horror, isn't he?' he went on, his voice very calm and chatty. 'Still, hardly surprising when you think about it, I suppose. A boy needs his mum, doesn't he?'

'Hasn't he got one, then?' Wendy asked.

'She ran off,' he said.

'I've got a dad that ran off,' Wendy said, stroking Slinky's head between his eyes. The firefighter was on the same branch by now and inching his way towards her. Slinky tickled her ear with his tongue. 'He's hungry,' she said. 'I think he wants his mouse.'

The firefighter looked puzzled.

'You know that snake, don't you?' he said.

'Course I do,' said Wendy. 'He's called Slinky. He belongs to my grandad.'

'So, he's not poisonous, then?'

'No.'

'And he's not strangling you, then?'

'No,' said Wendy. 'You can stroke him if you like.'

'No, thank you.' The firefighter smiled. 'I think I'll just get you down. Can you manage the ladder?'

Wendy shook her head. 'My legs, they've gone all wobbly and I feel sick.'

'Over my shoulder, then,' he said. 'I'll give you a fireman's lift.'

All the way down Wendy kept her eyes closed. 'You sure this snake of yours is friendly?' the firefighter asked. 'He's giving me funny looks.'

'Quite sure,' said Wendy, and she squeezed her eyes even tighter shut.

Then her feet were on the ground and there were other arms around her and she could open her eyes. Everyone was cheering. Mrs Green was crying and Mrs Paterson was crying. They were all crying and laughing at the same time, and Wendy's wobbly legs began to feel better again.

Chapter Six

GRANDAD WAS WELL enough to come along
in a wheelchair for the Christmas Evening. He
wasn't at all cross about Slinky. Wendy told him
everything and he just laughed and laughed.
Wendy's mother pushed him around the school,
smiling proudly whenever anyone talked about
Wendy and how brave she'd been.

Slinky was the star of the show. Curled up in
his tank with his cast-off skin beside him, he
flicked his tongue at everyone and looked very
pleased with himself.

After a bit Wendy wandered off on her own. She liked being liked. She liked being noticed. Fame had been fun, but she'd had enough of it already. She sat down in a corner of the hall and ate her mince pie.

'Wendy?'

Wendy looked up. It was Simon McTavish.

'I've got something,' he said. It was a Christmas present.

'For me?' He nodded.

She took it and unwrapped it. It was a game of Snakes and Ladders.

'That's from my dad,' he mumbled. 'This is from me.'

He handed her a Christmas card. She opened it up. It said:

'Sorry for what I did. Happy Christmas. Love from Simon McTavish.'

When she looked up again, he had gone.

Grandad was up and about by Christmas. They had his cauliflower with their chicken for Christmas dinner, and played Snakes and Ladders all evening with Slinky wrapped around Wendy's neck. It was far and away the best Christmas she'd ever had.